A Song Full of Sky

For Spy, Banjo, Ella & Jazz
& for all our animal brothers & sisters
R.D

To my parents
B.T

ORCHARD BOOKS
First published in Great Britain in 2021
by The Watts Publishing Group

1 3 5 7 9 10 8 6 4 2

HB ISBN 978-1-40836-180-1   PB ISBN 978-1-40836-181-8

Printed and bound in China

Orchard Books
An imprint of Hachette Children's Group
Part of The Watts Publishing Group Limited
Carmelite House, 50 Victoria Embankment, London, EC4Y 0DZ

An Hachette UK Company
www.hachette.co.uk   www.hachettechildrens.co.uk

A Song Full of Sky

Ruth Doyle

Illustrated by Britta Teckentrup

ORCHARD

There's a bird
outside your window
with a song that's full of sky,
and it wonders why
you stay inside
when you are free to fly?

A playground of puzzles is waiting for you,
each feather and footprint, a half-hidden clue.
There are secrets to find – be still and peer closely.
Spy curious chrysalis, tight-wrapped and ghostly!

In the long jungle grasses, watch ants work and play.
Count button-bright beetles as they scuttle away.

Smell the sun on soft petals,
taste berries warm and sweet . . .

Feel the tickles of tadpoles
as the stream cools your feet.

Glimpse glittering cobwebs,
build a stick den, play free . . .

As the warm breeze,
the light leaves . . .

The soft floating bee.

Look up high,
watch the moving theatre of sky –
kaleidoscope pictures are galloping by!

See the owl surfing sky like a moon-dappled kite . . .

Horses racing the clouds with their manes catching light.

And if ever you're frazzled
with worry and doubt.
Don't hold onto your troubles,
turn fears inside-out!

Throw your cares to the wind
and whisper a wish.
Tell crickets your secrets,
swap stories with fish.

The sky doesn't care how you look, what you wear.

The wind whispers, *"You're perfect,"*

and ruffles your hair.

So be a friend of the earth, show others the way.

Share sunshine and starlight, each night and new day.

You are part of the wonder
and joy Nature brings,
of the beauty and magic
in all living things.

So join the bird outside your window,
sing your own song full of sky.
Then open the door,
run free and explore . . .

Go, stretch out
your wild wings . . .

and fly!